Dino FC

The MISSING FANS

KEITH BRUMPTON

USBORNE

First published in 2010 by Usborne Publishing Ltd., Usborne House,
83-85 Saffron Hill, London EC1N 8RT, England.
www.usborne.com

JF AMJJASOND/10 95834 ISBN 9781409504849
Printed in Reading, Berkshire, UK.

DINO FC

Dear Dino-soccer fan,
Welcome back to Rumbley Stadium. After last season's troubles, we're hoping for much better things this time round. This is my first full season in charge of the squad. I want us to play exciting, attacking football and maybe even win a trophy for the first time in the club's history (except for the wooden spoon which we've won quite often).

I hope it's going to be a spectacular season and that we'll give you lots to cheer about!

All the best

Terry Triceratops

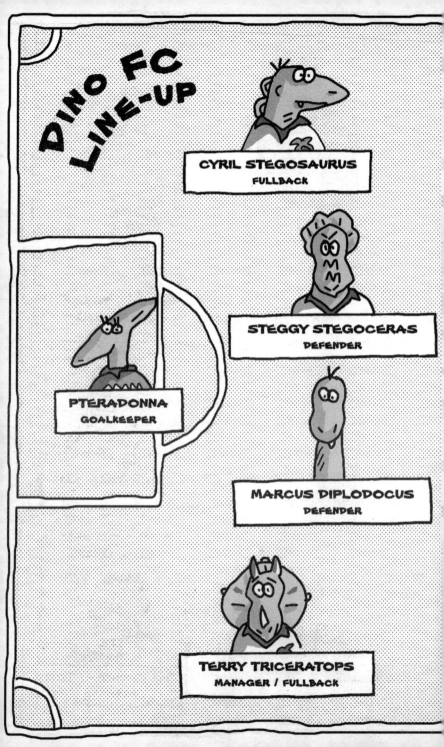

ARCHIE OPTERYX
LEFT WINGER

ALBERT ALLOSAURUS
CENTRE MIDFIELD

CELIA COELOPHYSIS
FORWARD

GWEN CORYTHOSAURUS
CENTRE MIDFIELD

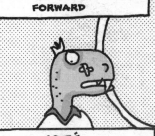

JOSÉ HETERODONTOSAURUS
FORWARD

ERIC ALLOSAURUS
RIGHT MIDFIELD

TODAY'S SUB:

OLLIE OVIRAPTOR
FORWARD

CHAPTER 1

Some football clubs have loads of money.
Some have a little bit of money. And some,
like Dino FC, have none.

Player-manager Terry Triceratops was
holding a crisis meeting with his loyal
number two and fellow fullback, Cyril
Stegosaurus.

glum
look

Being a stegosaurus, Cyril had very little grasp of figures.

"It means we're broke…" replied Terry, who was staring into an almost empty box marked "club funds".

In his second season in charge, young Terry was finding out that being the manager of a club with no money wasn't easy: Rumbley Stadium looked shabby because it hadn't been painted for a long time, and the grass on the pitch was growing out of control because the club couldn't afford to pay a groundsdinosaur to eat it. (Even though the team's tall but dim centre half, Marcus Diplodocus, had volunteered to graze it for free.)

But the biggest problem of all was that Terry didn't have any money to buy new players. Dino FC had a tiny squad of just twelve, and he worried about what would happen if anyone got injured or suspended.

He wouldn't even be able to fill the subs' bench! The argumentative Allosaurus brothers (who played in midfield) already had four yellow rocks each (one more and they'd be suspended for three matches).

Terry also knew that the team had been short of goals last season, and wished he had the funds to sign a new striker...

Terry had spotted a brilliant young
player he thought would get lots of goals
for them. His name was Dazza Dimetrodon.

Dazza played for a side called Atletico
Dimetrodon, and Terry thought he had great
potential: four fast feet, a well-balanced tail,
and a beady eye for goal. The only trouble
was, Atletico Dimetrodon knew Dazza had

ability and told Terry if he wanted to sign him it would cost 50,000 bushels.

Terry told Cyril the bad news about the price, but said that he thought Dazza was worth it. Cyril looked glum.

"Which he doesn't like spending," frowned Cyril.

Danny Deinonychus was well known as the meanest chairman in the Dino Premiership. He was so mean the team shared a towel between them and were the only club to have an unheated swamp bath.

But Terry could be a very determined triceratops when he put his mind to it.

WE MIGHT NOT BE ABLE TO AFFORD DAZZA AT THE MOMENT, BUT WHAT IF WE COULD PERSUADE MORE FANS TO COME TO OUR MATCHES?

Cyril could see what Terry meant. The more dinosaurs who paid to watch the team, the more money the club would have to spend.

But Cyril didn't think this plan would work. He couldn't see any more fans coming to watch. Because they'd lost so many matches over the years, Dino FC were now the worst supported team in the Dino Premiership, with an average attendance last season of just nine.

Cyril couldn't see how they were going to change that. But Terry had a gleam in his eye.

"There are thousands of potential fans out there. We just need to let them know we're here and that we're going to be playing great football. I'm talking *marketing*."

Cyril didn't know what marketing was exactly, but he didn't like the sound of it.

Terry suddenly looked very serious. "If we can't attract bigger crowds we won't be able to sign anyone. In fact, I'm worried Danny might shut the club down altogether!"

CHAPTER 2

After an early morning training session, Terry told his squad of players about his exciting plan.

"Why?" asked Steggy Stegoceras, the team's hard-headed defender. He always asked awkward questions.

"Because the boss wants to sign a brilliant new striker," Cyril blurted out, "and the only way we can afford him is to raise more money from ticket sales."

On hearing the news that a new player might be joining them, the whole squad suddenly looked upset and began to argue among themselves.

Soon the whole team was squabbling over whose place was most at risk.

Terry had to bang his tail on the ground
to restore order.

The hubbub died down.

LOOK, WHETHER I SIGN A
NEW PLAYER OR NOT, YOU'RE
ALL STILL PART OF MY PLANS
FOR THE TEAM AND THAT'S NOT
GOING TO CHANGE.

"I want to attract new fans," he
continued, "not just to raise money, but
because we're going to be playing great
football this season and I want more
dinosaurs to see it."

NICE
ONE.

Celia liked the sound of that – she had an eye for celebrity and always appreciated a big audience.

Even grumpy Steggy Stegoceras began to think it would be cool if more fans could watch his top-class performances.

It was then that Terry finally revealed his plan...

CHAPTER 3

Later that day, Eric and Albert Allosaurus visited Triassic Park Primary School. This was the first part of Terry's scheme – to get some of his players to visit local schools, sign a few autographs, and encourage the kids to come and watch Dino FC play their next game.

Unfortunately, the visit wasn't going too well. Eric and Albert had begun by quarrelling over whose autograph the kids would want most, and ended up rolling on the floor of the classroom, fighting and biting.

The class teacher had no alternative but to tell Eric and Albert that they were very naughty and make them go and stand outside the room.

Terry had to go to the school and apologize for the brothers' behaviour. It wasn't a good start to his campaign to find more fans. He hoped the next part of his scheme would be more successful!

Terry had sent Marcus Diplodocus to the busiest street in the valley, on a mission to persuade anyone he found there to come and watch Dino FC play.

Marcus soon found himself among a busy crowd of dinosaurs.

Big Marcus was a shy dinosaur who didn't like being the centre of attention. He didn't want to let his manager down, but how could he persuade anyone to come and watch Dino FC play? Marcus desperately tried to think of something.

He wasn't the most skilful player in the team — he didn't go in for tricks and ball juggling like Archie or Celia — his style was more about barging the opposition off the ball and thumping the ball high over the stands. But a bit of keepy-uppy might be just the thing to impress the crowd, he decided.

Marcus began balancing a football on the end of his very large feet and then switched to keepy-uppy.

ONE...

TWO...

THREE...

THUMP

WHOOPS!

OH, NO!

Marcus's fourth touch was a little heavy. Well actually it was *very* heavy. The ball had ricocheted off his foot and into a nearby tree. It struck with such force that the tree snapped clean in two and fell. The watching crowd ran for cover as the huge tree crashed to the ground and lay there, blocking the whole road. There was chaos!

Marcus soon found himself surrounded by a mob of angry, grumbling dinosaurs:

It was lucky Terry arrived in time to sort

things out.

He got Marcus and a couple of strong dinosaurs to drag the tree from the road, then calmed down the angry crowd by promising them free tickets to the next match.

Free tickets! It was the exact OPPOSITE of what he'd planned. The club was still broke and his dream of signing a new player seemed further away than ever!

Later, Terry bumped into the club's grumpy defender, Steggy Stegoceras. Steggy had heard the news about the road blockage and the Allosaurus brothers getting into trouble. He shook his head gloomily.

"This team is better at annoying people than persuading them to come to matches. Face it, your plan is doomed."

But Terry was still hopeful. He told Steggy he'd asked Ollie Oviraptor, elderly striker and one of the most sensible members of the team, to open a club stall outside the ground.

"Autographs? Nobody will want autographs from that rabble!" sniffed Steggy.

Terry hoped Steggy was wrong. This was the club's last chance to raise the much-needed cash.

Ollie had set up his stall in the shadow of Mount Rumble itself.

As Terry drew close to the ground he got very excited. There were crowds of dinosaurs everywhere, and for once they all looked very happy.

When he arrived at the stall, it seemed every single piece of Dino FC merchandise had sold out – in fact there was nothing left at all. Terry shook Ollie by the claw.

Terry still looked delighted.

Terry couldn't believe what he was hearing. "Nothing? But I saw everyone going home with club souvenirs. What happened?"

Ollie reluctantly explained that the first dinosaur to show up was a young euparkeria and she told him she couldn't afford anything because she hardly got any pocket money. Ollie felt sorry for her and gave her one or two things for free.

Before he knew it, the young dinosaur had told everyone that the souvenirs were free and soon there was a huge queue.

Ollie couldn't charge money because there would have been a riot.

Terry sat down on a nearby rock. He felt very low.

It didn't look like Terry would be signing Dazza any time soon. They had spent a whole day trying to raise the profile of the club and attract new fans, but it seemed all they'd actually done was annoy the whole neighbourhood and give away the entire contents of the club stall!

Tomorrow was match day, so it was time to forget about attracting new fans for now, and concentrate on winning. It was going to be a very tough game – against Atletico Dimetrodon.

Dino FC were the home team but you
would never have guessed it from the crowd
gathering on the way to Rumbley Stadium.
All you could see were Atletico fans wearing
their red and white scarves and shirts.

"I wish we had that kind of support," grumbled Steggy, pulling on his shorts.

"So that plan to get bigger crowds was a complete waste of time? I always said it was doomed. Doomed," wailed Steggy.

The rest of the team began adding their own thoughts and Cyril had to calm them down so Terry could begin his prematch team talk.

LISTEN UP, GUYS...

THIS WILL BE A WASTE OF TIME!

Terry had been working on his talk all morning, but the team found it hard to hear him above the chanting of the Atletico fans.

"Attack at the drop of a hat," Ollie thought he heard the boss say. But actually, Terry had said, "*Don't* attack too much, I want you to drop back."

EH?

In fact, as the team ran out to start the match, not one of them had heard Terry's instructions properly.

MUST GET MY EARS TESTED NEXT WEEK.

So it wasn't surprising that they quickly got themselves into a muddle. Eric and Albert Allosaurus both thought Terry had said *they* could take the corners and got a warning from the ref for arguing with each other.

Ollie Oviraptor played the whole of the first half in attack, when Terry had really wanted him to drop into midfield.

And the Atletico Dimetrodon fans were shouting so loudly that when Terry tried to change things on the pitch he still couldn't make himself understood.

Dino FC almost held out until just before half-time, but then a long, high ball bounced into their penalty area.

Marcus Diplodocus shouted, "Mine!" but Pteradonna, the team's brilliant young goalie, couldn't hear him above the din, and tried to catch the ball.

I'VE GOT IT!

THUMP!

They collided with each other and the Atletico centre forward had the easiest of tasks to tap the ball into an empty net.

It was Dazza Dimetrodon, the youngster Terry had wanted to sign.

The second half was no better for Dino FC. Dazza Dimetrodon ran rings around Terry and his defence. And then he ran squares around them. And then triangles.

The full-time whistle blew loudly in Celia's ear, as the game ended with a five-nil win to Atletico Dimetrodon.

Terry felt very gloomy, and not just because the lava showers were freezing cold (due to an unpaid heating bill).

"That was a disaster! A home match and we couldn't even hear our own fans," he groaned.

"I heard someone shouting 'rubbish'," interrupted Steggy, unhelpfully.

"The fans we do have probably won't be coming back after that," admitted Terry. "I don't know what more we can do."

The team's young goalie, Pteradonna didn't often say much – she was usually too busy practising her goalkeeping. But she raised her wing, and told Terry she might have an idea.

Pteradonna didn't seem fazed. "I know a way we can advertise for nothing, and no one will be able to ignore it."

Terry asked her what she meant.

"We fly a banner across the sky," continued the young goalkeeper. "We can make one to publicize our next match, and Archie and me can fly it around the valley."

WICKED! COUNT ME IN.

"But what would we put on it?" asked Marcus, who wasn't very good at thinking up plans.

"How about 'Support your local team'," suggested Gwen, drying herself with a large leaf.

"And we could offer all tickets half price," added Terry, excitedly. "That's bound to get new fans in!"

Early next morning, Pteradonna and Archie Opteryx flew off into a brilliant golden sky, each of them clutching one end of the banner between their beaks. It felt very heavy at first and it looked like they might not be able to stay airborne.

But gradually they climbed higher and higher, until they reached a warm, thermal breeze on which they could glide.

The banner's message was written in large black letters, and could be clearly seen from the ground. Pteradonna and Archie flew over the whole valley just to be sure no one missed them.

The flying banner wasn't the only Dino FC stunt to happen that day. Celia and Gwen had volunteered to visit Muddy Swamp Shopping Centre to sign autographs and talk about their lives as footballers. The large crowd seemed very excited by the whole event, and this time neither dinosaur forgot to remind everyone about coming to support Dino FC.

Terry was delighted at the way his players had rallied round. But with the next game in two days' time, he was still worried. Would the locals turn up – or stay at home watching "Celebrity Ballroom Dino-Dancing" instead?

On the eve of the match, Dino FC trained hard under Terry's watchful eye. Even injury-prone José Heterodontosaurus turned out, despite a sprained eyebrow.

Their next fixture was a derby match against Plesiosaur City. It would be exciting – the sort of match that should attract a big crowd...

Terry spent a restless night. He had a nightmare that he'd slept in and that the game had started without him. By the time he'd got to the ground and changed into his strip the match had finished and the ground was empty.

He woke with a start, not sure whether he'd just been dreaming or whether he really *had* missed the match. He was relieved to see the sun coming up over Mount Rumble.

On his way to the ground, Terry was hoping to see a few home supporters, but the road was empty, except for Cyril, who Terry could see waiting for him up ahead.

NO SIGN OF ANY NEW FANS!

"Still, early days, they'll come..." answered Terry, trying to sound more cheerful than he actually felt.

Outside Rumbley Stadium the only fans in view were those from Plesiosaur City. They were slapping their flippers together and chanting their team song:

There must have been a thousand of them, all crowding into the visitors' end.

Inside the Dino FC dressing cave the team pulled on their kit and limbered up.

Terry's team talk was quite short by his usual standards – only about twenty minutes. Nineteen of those minutes were taken up trying, yet again, to explain the offside rule to Marcus Diplodocus (who had two brains, neither of which were very big).

Convinced he had finally got through to Marcus, Terry turned his attention to tactics for the match itself.

"It's a must-win game," he announced.

"A must-win game," repeated Cyril, keen that no one should miss the boss's words.

"Let's take it easy for the first ten minutes," Terry continued, "lots of tight marking and lots of talking."

Steggy Stegoceras rolled his eyes. There was no time for Terry to explain that by "talking" he meant telling your teammates what was happening around them.

"Just remember," Terry called out, "we might not have many fans but we play for the club. We play for each other."

The team ran out from their dressing cave towards the pitch. As they emerged they could hear a strange noise growing

around them. It was like a distant roar.
Surely Mount Rumble wasn't erupting
again? Terry hated playing on the pitch
when it was covered in hot lava.

But the sound the team was hearing
wasn't the nearby volcano, it was the
packed home stand, full of Dino FC fans!

Terry and his team couldn't believe it. One side of the ground was completely full – a mass of yellow and blue scarves, ticker tape and singing spectators.

Celia Coelophysis wished she'd spent more time on her make-up. José Heterodontosaurus's agent decided he'd have to demand extra appearance money for his client. Even Marcus Diplodocus noticed something different.

And the extra home fans certainly affected Terry. He'd never played in front of so many of them before. Thousands of away fans screaming for their own team, yes – but a big home crowd all expecting the team to win – no! He suddenly felt very nervous. His throat went dry and his legs turned to jelly. He had to check that the ground wasn't moving beneath him. It wasn't – he was just feeling dizzy.

The referee blew his nose (he didn't have a whistle) and Terry shook the flipper of the Plesiosaur City captain. It had started raining, which would suit the visitors – they loved wet conditions.

"Isn't that crowd great?" said Cyril Stegosaurus, not noticing that his boss now looked very nervous and shaky.

"Uh, yeah...great," answered Terry, not marking City's left winger, who took the ball from a quick throw-in, raced round Terry, and fired in a fierce shot. Pteradonna got a claw to the ball but couldn't stop it hitting the back of the net.

missed tackle

stunned silence

THAT WAS MY FAULT.

Terry had put all that effort into trying to fill the ground with home supporters but now he'd succeeded, it seemed he was too nervous to play in front of them!

Gwen Corythosaurus laid a webbed claw on Terry's shoulder.

The game resumed, with Cyril wondering why Terry was feeling so edgy. More importantly, he wondered if there was anything he could do to help his boss defeat his nerves – before they cost the team this vital match.

As half-time arrived, and with Dino FC still losing one-nil, Cyril grabbed Terry's arm and led him to one side of the dressing cave.

SOMETHING'S WRONG, BOSS, AND WE'VE GOT FIFTEEN MINUTES TO FIND OUT WHAT'S MAKING YOU SO NERVOUS...

Terry nodded. He wanted to know too. Cyril asked if Terry had ever had a bad experience playing at Rumbley Stadium?

Terry's mind flashed back to a school game he'd played in, years earlier. It was the final of the Inter-School's Trophy and, with the scores level, Terry's team had been awarded a penalty. While the rest of the team could hardly bear to look, Terry had stepped confidently up to take the kick. He'd never missed a penalty in his young life. But as he ran in, his hoof scuffed a large stone and he blasted the ball high over the bar.

Terry looked suddenly pale as he told Cyril what had happened next. "Some of the mums and dads in the crowd started to shout at me. They said I was useless and that I'd let the team down. I remember my legs turned to jelly. Just like they did today. For

the rest of that game I played the worst
football I ever played in my life."

Cyril frowned. The reason why Terry
had been playing so badly was now clear.
"You're scared the fans watching us could
turn against you, like those folks who booed
you all those years ago."

Terry nodded.

BUT OUR FANS WOULDN'T
DO THAT. THEY WANT YOU
TO PLAY WELL.

Terry felt a little better. Cyril was right.
The home crowd didn't want Dino FC to
lose. They didn't want him to play badly.
They wanted to see their team play some
great football with energy and passion. And
that's just what they were going to get!

Terry told the team he wanted them to forget the first half...

I ALREADY HAVE.

...Dino FC were going to grab all three points and send their fans home with something to sing about.

Steggy said they'd be lucky, but the rest of the team looked up for it.

The second half got under way with Plesiosaur City back on the attack.

WATCH OUT, GAFFER!

Terry heard Gwen's call and expertly took the ball out of the air before striking a lovely pass through to Eric Allosaurus in midfield.

Eric skipped a couple of tackles and hit a ferocious shot into the top right corner.

After his talk with Cyril, Terry now knew why he was nervous in front of the home fans. He'd never got over missing that penalty all those years ago. He was annoyed with himself for being so silly.

"A good boss never makes the same mistake twice," he remembered an old manager telling him.

A determined triceratops on the rampage is quite a sight. And Terry Triceratops was now feeling *very* determined. The fans had filled the ground to support him and the team – they wanted him to succeed, not fail!

determined
look

The longer the game went on, the less nervous Terry felt. The rest of the team were responding to the home fans too. Archie went through his whole array of tricks: juggling, nutmegging, sitting on the ball and generally teasing the opposition.

Centre half Marcus won every header; and Pteradonna caught crosses like she was grabbing a fish for supper.

But with just one minute to go it was still one-all. Would Dino FC settle for a draw? No way! Terry shouted to Cyril that he was pushing himself up into attack in a last ditch bid to win the game...

CHAPTER 11

Dino FC won a free kick after a plesiosaur flattened José Heterodontosaurus with an outstretched flipper. José rolled over about fifty times and told the ref he thought he might have to go off.

Eric Allosaurus was a free-kick specialist (or so he kept telling his brother). But Albert insisted that he wasn't.

While they argued, quick-thinking Terry stepped up and hit a high, floating ball into the box. The ball hung in the air and big Marcus Diplodocus tried to head it.

But before he could get there, a plesiosaur flipper shot up and punched the ball away from him.

The referee agreed and pointed straight to the penalty spot.

The Dino FC crowd went wild. Terry could hear them. They thought the game was already won.

But Terry knew a penalty kick doesn't count as a goal until the ball hits the back of the net. He took the ball from the ref and placed it on the smudge of chalk that was the penalty spot.

"Are you sure you don't want me to take it?" asked Steggy. "You look very nervous."

Terry looked at Cyril, then shook his head.

The Plesiosaur keeper was waving his flippers around to try and put Terry off.

Terry felt his nerves beginning to return. But then he remembered his half-time chat with Cyril. He'd missed a penalty all those years ago and had let it bother him ever since. Time to change all that!

The ref blew his nose. This would be the last kick of the match. The crowd fell silent. All eight thousand of them.

Terry focused on the ball and decided exactly where he was going to hit it. He could almost hear his own hooves as they glided across the damp grass.

Terry struck the ball to the left. It hit the post and rebounded into the back of the net, via the Plesiosaur goalie's head.

Dino FC had won two-one! The three points were theirs!

The home fans went crazy, jumping up and down and chanting Terry's name:

As Terry waved to them, he thought he must have the best job in the world.

CHAPTER 12

"We made three thousand bushels today, thanks to all those extra fans," announced Cyril, as he finally finished counting the gate money. The other Dino FC players were delighted at the news.

"Nice one," announced Danny Deinonychus, the club chairman who'd just entered the dressing cave. "I'd best look after that," he said, grabbing the cash and putting it into his briefcase.

Before anyone could protest he was off.

Terry looked around the dressing cave at his team, who were totally exhausted after the match. They were a good bunch and they had given everything to win the three points. Terry made an announcement.

Everyone cheered. Even Steggy.

While the rest of the team got showered and changed, Terry left to sign autographs for some young fans who had gathered outside the dressing cave.

YOU'RE A GREAT PLAYER. I WISH I COULD TAKE PENALTIES LIKE YOU. I MISSED ONE LAST WEEK.

Terry smiled at the youngster. "Everyone misses a penalty at some stage of their career. The thing is not to let it bother you. Just keep doing your best."

As the young triceratops nodded, Terry grabbed a ball from his bag.

The young Dino fans couldn't believe their ears.

So, as the sun went down and the ground slowly emptied, Terry Triceratops helped the youngsters practise their skills until there was no more light to play by.

SEE YOU AT THE NEXT MATCH, MR. TRICERATOPS.

Terry smiled. It looked like the team had a bunch of young fans who would be supporting them for a long time to come...

THE END

MEET THE PLAYERS IN DINO FC

– THE CRAZIEST TEAM IN THE JURASSIC WORLD!

RUMBLEY STADIUM – THE DINO FC GROUND

PTERADONNA **1**

POSITION: goalkeeper
SKILLS: flying
LIKES: catching crosses
DISLIKES: non-football days
FOOTY FACT: the youngest member of the squad

STEGGY STEGOCERAS **2**

POSITION: defender
SKILLS: good at marking opponents
LIKES: grumbling
DISLIKES: being told what to do
FOOTY FACT: applied for the manager's job but Terry got it

MARCUS DIPLODOCUS **3**

POSITION: defender
SKILLS: great in the air
LIKES: heading the ball
DISLIKES: quick forwards
FOOTY FACT: last season won 76% of all headers

TERRY TRICERATOPS **4**

POSITION: manager and fullback
SKILLS: tactician
LIKES: tough talking
DISLIKES: defensive football
FOOTY FACT: only player-manager in the DPL

CYRIL STEGOSAURUS 5

POSITION: fullback

SKILLS: following instructions

LIKES: moving slowly

DISLIKES: anyone criticizing Terry, "the boss"

FOOTY FACT: the vice-captain

ALBERT ALLOSAURUS 6

POSITION: midfield

SKILLS: dealing with tricky forwards

LIKES: arguing with his twin

DISLIKES: Eric. Refs

FOOTY FACT: once got 21 red cards in a season

GWEN CORYTHOSAURUS 7

POSITION: midfield

SKILLS: controlling midfield

LIKES: playing in the rain

DISLIKES: hot temperatures

FOOTY FACT: the team's free kick specialist

ARCHIE OPTERYX 8

POSITION: winger

SKILLS: great dribbler

LIKES: doing ball tricks

DISLIKES: bumpy pitches

FOOTY FACT: takes the team's corners

ERIC ALLOSAURUS 9

POSITION: midfield
SKILLS: tackling, marking
LIKES: arguing with his twin
DISLIKES: Albert. Refs
FOOTY FACT: once got 20 red cards in a season

CELIA COELOPHYSIS 10

POSITION: forward
SKILLS: fast and graceful
LIKES: looking good on the pitch
DISLIKES: tackling or being tackled
FOOTY FACT: fastest player on the team

JOSÉ HETERODONTOSAURUS 11

POSITION: forward
SKILLS: falling over in the box
LIKES: winning penalties
DISLIKES: most things
FOOTY FACT: on average only fit for 2.3 games per season

OLLIE OVIRAPTOR 12

POSITION: utility player
SKILLS: football brain, experience
LIKES: resting after the match
DISLIKES: playing 90 minutes
FOOTY FACT: has been a pro for 22 seasons

9781409504832

Coming soon...

9781409504856

9781409504863

For more action-packed reads head to

WWW.FICTION.USBORNE.COM